FOLLOW THE GREEN LINE

William Payne King, M.D.

Copyright © 2003 by William Payne King, M.D.

Library of Congress Number:		2003092911
ISBN:	Hardcover	1-4010-8496-6
	Softcover	1-4010-8495-8

All rights reserved. No part of this book may be reproduced or transmitted in any form or by any means, electronic or mechanical, including photocopying, recording, or by any information storage and retrieval system, without permission in writing from the copyright owner.

This is a work of fiction. Names, characters, places and incidents either are the product of the author's imagination or are used fictitiously, and any resemblance to any actual persons, living or dead, events, or locales is entirely coincidental, except as explained in the Foreword.

This book was printed in the United States of America.

To order additional copies of this book, contact:
Xlibris Corporation
1-888-795-4274
www.Xlibris.com
Orders@Xlibris.com

17252-KING

CONTENTS

Credits 7
Foreword 11

Chapter One
   The Prelude 13
Chapter Two
   Gailor 21
Chapter Three
   Medicine 26
Chapter Four
   Obstetrics and Gynecology 38
Chapter Five
   Pediatrics 60
Chapter Six
   General Surgery 66
Chapter Seven
   Psychiatry 73
Chapter Eight
   Emergency Room 81
Chapter 9
   Epilogue 91

Biography
   William Payne King, M.D. 95

Credits

Photographs—

Photographs numbers 1, 2, 3, 4, 5 and 6, courtesy of Memphis/Shelby County Public Library and Information Center

Front cover photograph, plus photographs numbers 7, 8, 9 and 10, courtesy of Memphis/Shelby County Public Library and Information Center—Shultz Collection.

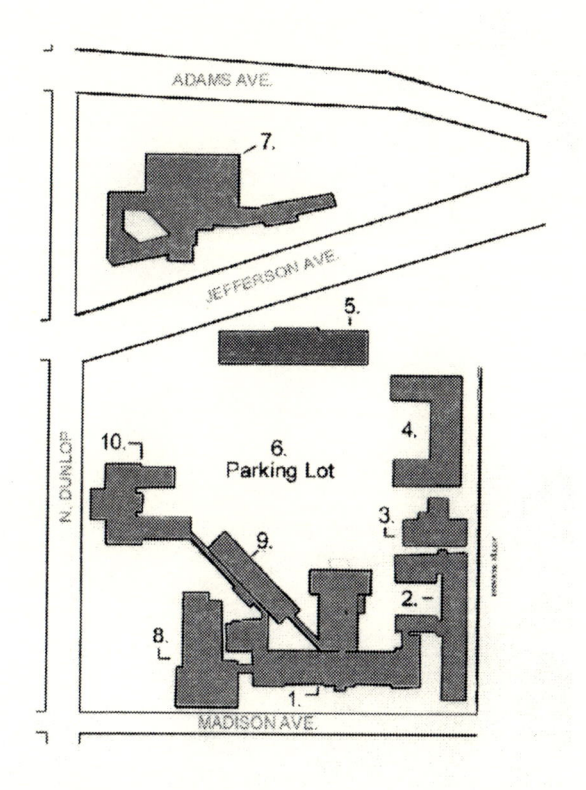

Legend
John Gaston Medical Complex

1. John Gaston Hospital
2. Maternity Ward
3. University of Tennessee Laboratory
4. Nurses Residence
5. Isolation Hospital
6. Parking Lot
7. West Tennessee Tuberculosis Hospital
8. University of Tennessee Institute of Pathology
9. Frank Tobey Pediatric Center
10. Thomas F. Gailor Diagnostic Clinic and Psychiatric Center

FOREWORD

The contents of this book are based generally on my recollections of surroundings, circumstances, and attitudes as they existed during my internship in the mid-1950s at John Gaston Hospital, Memphis, Tennessee. Other than family and myself, the characters are fictional. They represent a collage of many friends, associates, patients and acquaintances. All anecdotal stories are based on either my or a comrade's personal remembrances. An occasional factual detail may be altered for literary purposes, or, very possibly, because of a nearly half-century mental lapse. When so, mea culpa!

To those of you who were either there or in a similar circumstance during those times, there is nothing new in this offering except, perhaps, nostalgia. But for the rest of you, the vast majority, welcome to a whole new world that really did exist in the not-too-distant past. Special appreciation is extended to the many classmates and their spouses who, like me, poked way back in their gray matter and helped with forgotten pieces of the puzzle

Also, many thanks to all those at the University of Tennessee Center for Health Science, especially

Bill Robinson, the Memphis/Shelby County Public Library, especially Patricia M. LaPointe, and the *Memphis Commercial Appeal* newspaper, especially Mike Kerr, who graciously contributed their time and energy to help make this book a reality. Also, my gratitude to Richard Raichelson, my assistant researcher, and photographer Robert Dye for jobs well done.

CHAPTER ONE

The Prelude

My curriculum vitae states, for college, "A.B. Duke University, 1951"; for medical school, "M.D. University of Tennessee, December 1954". Why designate the month for medical school and not for college? Everyone knows the academic year ends in late May or early June, so if I didn't note the month of medical school graduation, it might appear my medical education spanned a mere three years. Nay, tain't so! But, "graduation in December" alerts the reader that something here is amiss.

And, indeed, it was. Being a state institution of higher learning, the goal at hand was to produce baseline physicians for community service as efficiently as possible. Specialty training was not put forth as a primary goal, and "research" was no goal at all. So, instead of taking off the summer for a breather, we plunged rapidly forward on the quarter system, one quarter consisting of a three-month period, taking off but one quarter at the halfway mark. Thus, we have graduation in December rather than June.

Of course, at that time the community had to wait for the services of the newly produced docs, because after the usual year of internship, if you could breathe, at least two years of armed service duty awaited. Ah, but that's another story for later telling.

I was born a 1929 Depression baby in Memphis. My father when a young bachelor was a local professional boxer. He quit the ring after fighting to a draw with a well-known fighter one weight heavier, figuring if he didn't win, then he wasn't good enough to continue in that business. He then moved to Chicago, worked in the daytime for Dr. Scholl's selling shoes, and went to Chiropody school at night to become a foot doctor. He opened an office of Chiropody, now known as Podiatry, next to the shoe department in Goldsmith's Department Store, where he practiced for many years before relocating to a private office building.

My mother was of Italian-father-English-mother descent. In those earliest remembrances of childhood, I recall living with my mother's parents on Dickinson Street. I can still hear the exuberant cries of triumph and anguish from the family as they played pinochle on a large green wooden table over my head.

Before I attended grammar school we moved into our first house a few blocks away on Willett, where we lived until shortly before high school. The house was strictly middle class—you know, one bathroom, one car, an icebox that required a "sure-nuff" block of ice, et al.

At birth I presented breach, that is, feet first, "tearing her up," as momma would say, so she couldn't have any more children. Some say I've been ass-first ever since. Those days, especially in the South, it was unseemly for the woman of the house to occupy herself with any other duties than being a wife, mother, and home keeper. Thus, while I never would have lacked for love, attention and life's essentials, Duke University, in all probability, would have been too much of a financial strain if I had not been an only child.

I had applied to two medical schools, the elite Duke, which took only forty-five or so new students each year, and my home-state school, which accepted a similar number every quarter. While I was accepted as a high alternate at Duke, assuring a place if not that year then the next, I was accepted straight off for the September class at Tennessee.

Not only was Tennessee a medical school with an excellent reputation, but also it was in my hometown, Memphis. The financial advantages of home-state school tuition, plus those of living at home, were obvious. Oh yes, there was another eminent factor on the horizon, Korea. If I could get through medical school, I would at least go as an "officer and a gentleman" in the Medical Corps. Remember *MASH*?

And, one more small consideration! While at Duke I sort of got emotionally entangled with this girl, another pre-med student in my class. Well, the combination of twenty-two-year-old hormones and the scruples of the early 1950s resulted in the same old dilemma that has plagued countless lovebirds. So, of course, after I was accepted to medical school, we did the "sensible" thing. We got married and built a small living room addition to my parent's house. My father generously agreed to provide the same small allowance through medical school that I received in college and we just assumed everything would work out. Ah, youth!

With my bride's Bachelor of Science degree in Zoology from Duke, she was able to get a small paying job in a nearby private hospital as a medical technician, where she achieved her official Medical Technology Certification while on the job. Her contribution not only helped put food on our table at that time, but also later proved invaluable when I was in private practice many years later and had to meet new and tougher personnel qualification requirements to maintain an office laboratory. My wife once again came to the rescue. It must be true: God takes care of fools and drunks, because here we are, over fifty-one years later, with four children and six grandchildren.

The trials and tribulations of medical school have been examined and dissected so many times elsewhere, I shall forego them here. I will note, however, the arrival of a baby girl during the last year of medical school. While it was a joyous occasion, it did put a major crimp in the family income for a while. Thank God for grandmothers.

Then, at long last, the class of December 1954 stood in the school auditorium in our black robes and doctoral hoods, the latter trimmed in Medicine's forest green velvet, and lined on the inside with the orange-and-white colors of the University of Tennessee. Being proclaimed a "doctor," indeed, was a treasured moment. At that time the title identified not just a profession, but also a vocation—a vocation with a built-in dedication to responsibility and duty, above all else, even family. It is unfortunate that present-day social and financial upheavals have brought about regrettable change in this noble mindset.

But while we all felt the exuberance of "no more teachers, no more books," it would not be long before the stark reality of internship would soon serve as a cold shower. Before becoming a practicing physician, by law in most states (though not then in Tennessee), the graduating M.D. must complete this "initiation." Why this "loophole" in Tennessee state law existed I am not sure—probably to allow a more prompt provision of needed medical services to rural locales. I cannot recall, however, any of my fellow students going directly into practice after graduation. At any rate, the completion of an internship program was certainly a must if a specialty residency was ever to be considered. Paradoxically, the more brutal the internship program, the greater the prestige, and, oh yes, the less the pay!

The internship at the University of Tennessee

teaching hospital John Gaston, better known to us as the Johnnie G., was considered very prestigious! From the yearly graduating class of approximately 180 new physicians, 3 rotating internships a month, 36 a year, were available. I, along with a December '54 classmate and a March '55 graduate, was accepted to begin the program in March '55.

John Gaston Hospital was officially opened and dedicated on June 27, 1936 at its 860 Madison Avenue location. It replaced a sorely outdated, inadequate, deteriorating three-story Memphis General Hospital that had existed at that site since 1898. The proud new building presented a 252-foot front, and was 76 feet wide. It had a brick face, was six-stories-plus-basement high, and was attractively complimented with a terraced entrance.

At that time it was truly the pride and joy of the city. It was claimed to be one of, if not *the* most, up-to-date and beautiful hospital in the South. It had large spacious wards housing 22 beds each, complete with ceiling fans and southern exposure windows, air-conditioned modern surgery suites, and the very latest X-ray equipment. The new hospital, according to a 1936 *Memphis Commercial Appeal* newspaper story, would provide for 550 patients.

The service wing of the main hospital, which housed the kitchens, cafeteria, and such, extended directly back from the center of the main building, much as the leg of the letter "T." The "receiving ward," better known as the emergency room, with its covered ambulance entrance was on the first floor at the tail end of the service wing.

It is of some interest that the old Memphis General Hospital, which was built on land originally utilized by the Catholic Church for an orphanage and cemetery, had itself replaced a totally dilapidated, vermin-filled two-story 1845 Memphis City Hospital of Civil War vintage. That hospital had been located on a ten-acre plot just one block west on the other side of Madison Avenue on land later converted into a wooded city "Forrest Park." The park was named in honor of the Civil War Confederate Cavalry hero Nathan Bedford Forrest. He and his wife are buried there beneath a statue of the general on horseback. It is somewhat incongruous that this park is the site of occasional racial demonstrations, the general being one of the original founders as well as a Supreme Grand Wizard of the Ku Klux Klan, an organization he claimed to later denounce.

The primary stimulus for the construction of this newest hospital was a 1929 donation of $300,000-plus home and furnishings in the will of Mrs. Theresa Gaston Mann. The donation was made in memory of her late first husband, her previous stepfather, John Gaston. With wise handling and major additional contributions from city, county and federal government sources, this sum grew over the next few years to $800,000.

John Gaston was a French immigrant who labored at New York's Delmonico's restaurant for three years before trying his hand at other miscellaneous endeavors. He made his fortune as a Memphis restaurateur and hotel proprietor before his death in 1912 at 84 years.

So, after a little post-graduation rest, I finally graduated from the white short jacket of the senior clinical medical student to the starched white shirt and pants of a John Gaston intern, along with the resulting groin chap. One of my fellow intern classmates did manage to avoid that indignity, her skirt sparing her the daily "rub." Of the three girls originally in our medical class, Jennifer Johnson, better known to us as J.J., was the only one to complete an internship. Nowadays, it would not be unusual to see nearly half of a medical school graduating class composed of female students. Life marches on.

CHAPTER TWO

Gailor

As is the usual growth patterns of such institutions, the John Gaston medical complex had expanded considerably when we arrived as interns in 1955. It now included a maternity wing to the east, and behind this the University of Tennessee Laboratory and the Marcus Haase Nurses Residence. To the west was built the University of Tennessee Institute of Pathology.

The old Isolation Hospital building was located across the parking area behind on the next street north, Jefferson. Sitting diagonally just west of the service wing was the Frank Tobey Pediatric Center, connected by a first-floor corridor to both the main hospital in front, and to the Thomas F. Gailor Hospital, the main topic of this paragraph, at the rear.

As earlier discussed, the prime purpose of this medical complex was care of the indigent medically ill of the then 400,000 Memphis citizens and, as much as facilities allowed, of surrounding Shelby County, Tennessee. To accomplish this feat, two necessities had to be adequately provided: the required plant and an adequate professional staff. Administration responsibilities, as designated in an official agreement formalized in 1926, were divided—the city taking care of the business end, and the university the professional aspects. We, being professional participants, were involved only with the latter, and left all the red tape to the pencil pushers, and welcome to it. Such policy was pretty standard throughout the complex, except for one strange exception, outpatient clinic admissions!

There existed only two standard paths to gain admission into John Gaston, the outpatient clinic and the emergency room. Very rarely did there occur a private patient admission. By far the great majority of admissions came through the John Gaston Outpatient Department, which was located on the first four floors of the Gailor Hospital building. The Gailor Psychiatric Hospital utilized the basement and the top floors. Pretty cozy, but somehow it all worked out.

The Director of the John Gaston Outpatient Department was the one and only city-paid physician. In addition to his duties as administrative supervisor, he personally screened and assigned clinics to all new outpatients or old outpatients with new ills.

Considering over 500 patients per day were seen in this clinic, one can readily appreciate the occasional chaos! In the clinics, medical students performed nearly all initial physical examinations, The John Gaston house staff, interns and residents, or rarely a faculty physician, saw them only after triage by the students, and never as a personal doctor.

In a May 1955 survey report the following statistics were provided for the previous year: The Outpatient Department provided for 154,703 visits, of which 15,074 were new patients and 111,958 were returns. Of this number 13,832 were to accomplish blood testing only. The vast majority of visits were handled in the day clinics as opposed to the night clinic, 126,393 to 13,839. Seventy-four percent were black patients and 16 percent were white. Sixty-five percent were female, 35 percent males.

There were three clinic sessions each day, morning, afternoon and night. All patients not before interviewed had to be pre-scrutinized for eligibility, and those without a prior appointment to a specific clinic appropriately assigned. Prior to proceeding to their particular clinic, a visit to the cash register must be made to pay the required 50-cent fee.

All of these pre-service chores were hopefully accomplished in a two-hour time period, allowing morning clinics to commence their professional activities by 10 A.M., and the afternoon clinics by 2 P.M. Ditto activities for the night clinic. Just talking about it exhausts me.

The varieties of clinics available? Give a look. Antibiotic, Cancer, Cardiac, Dermatology, Diabetic, Otolaryngology, Eye, Gastrointestinal, General Pediatric Cardiac, Proctology, Psychiatric, General Surgery, Thoracic Surgery, Thyroid, and Urology. Whew!

One of my old classmates reminded me of the "Saly" line, which I guess I had blocked out. Every weekday morning, except for Wednesday, when medical grand rounds were held for the students over in the Pathology building, there was an unbelievably long waiting line to receive a "Salyrgan" mercurial diuretic injection. This injection was given by the medical students. The line would proceed down three flights of stairs from the third-floor medical clinic, out the side door to Dunlap on which Gailor faced, south to Madison, east past John Gaston to the next street, Pauline—all in all, approximately three blocks. This diuretic was effective and inexpensive, but could be quite toxic—in which case the students would fall back on the interns for help. With the later arrival of the better-tolerated thiazides, this medication was replaced.

You can readily see where and how lots of medical students were utilized. As for us, the rotating interns, we with our residents spent our clinic time serving the specialty on which we were currently rotating. Only the schedule changed. A consulting staff physician was available, but rarely utilized. As for the other "elective" specialty clinics, their specific residents manned them, with an occasional staff supervisor lending a hand.

Gailor was truly the sustainer, the feeder of the entire health service complex. It's where most of it all began. As such, it was a necessary part of your daily existence, even during those rare days you might not have been there in person.

The other primary source of inpatients, though to a much smaller extent, was the emergency room. From this source came the huge assortment of acute emergencies, trauma cases, urgent obstetrical patients, etc. But, we will talk about this whiz-bang E.R. service, the last on the intern's rotation, in a later chapter.

CHAPTER THREE

Medicine

Michael Tripoli was the classmate I told you about who started internship with me. Michael and I took our first step up the staff ladder in March. Although it was the lowest rung, it was a start. Mike had married Barbara in the last year of medical school, and a baby was now early on the way. Physically, under his blond crew cut, Mike was a bit short in stature and baby faced, but his presence was all man. While he was gregarious and good-natured, you could sense a smoldering fire in the hole. Being partial to white buck shoes, I told him he looked like a snowflake in his new pristine outfit. He thought that was pretty funny.

George Zimmer, a member of the newest graduating quarter, was the third member of our tenderfoot group. He was a few years older than Mike and me. He had been some sort of submariner in the Second World War, a quieter, more serious sort. Either *compadre* would be, as they say in the westerns, "fine to ride the river with."

A general rotating internship is designed to expose the neophyte doctor to the more common varieties of medical experience. So, you do exactly as it says, *rotate*, beginning with a three-month sojourn on the medical service. The exact details of duty rotation on this service remain a subject of debate, there being no official documentation, and my available comrades' recollections varying. By consensus, it was deduced the duty was every third night, and every third weekend. The first of the three months was spent in the outpatient department, with the night duty hours tending the night clinic. I have already talked at length about life at the "Gailor," so I shall forego further review of such here. The last two months on the service were spent on the inpatient wards, where we shall now focus our attention.

John Gaston Hospital was located on the north side of Madison Avenue, directly across the street from the Medical School. Administration and X-ray primarily occupied the first floor, with an orthopedic fracture room addition on the far west end. The medical wards were located on the second and third floors. Except for a few isolation rooms, all beds were on open wards.

The entire hospital was strictly segregated, whites from blacks, or, as was the more common vernacular at that time, colored. There were two wards for men to the left and two for women to the right. The white wards were on the second floor and the black wards on the third floor. The white patient population was much smaller than the black. While, as previously said, each ward was originally designed to house twenty-two beds, on the black wards the count often rose to thirty or more with beds in the aisles and halls.

Despite the crowded conditions on the black wards, they were more popular with the students and the staff. The white charity patients were generally more disgruntled and uncooperative. Rumor has it that some industrious students even offered to trade from the black to the white service for a financial consideration.

In the winter months, spring and fall it wasn't so bad, but the summer months could be killers. Picture, if you will, a filled-to-capacity open ward with an outside temperature of 100 or so degrees, no airconditioning, and only ceiling fans and southern-exposure open windows for cooling! One trick of the medical residents was to order oxygen tents for their heart patients, not because they needed oxygen, but for the cooling effect! Imagine collecting 24-hour urine specimens under the bed in such an environment. The human is truly a creature capable of remarkable adaptation.

My most "unfavorite" spot was a small makeshift laboratory on each floor. Here the intern or his assigned medical students performed "by hand" all of the mundane laboratory tests, such as urinalysis and complete blood counts (CBCs). There was present a microscope, slides and cover slips, test tubes and racks, hand counter and the now-unheard-of hemoglobinometer. I recently asked a young pathologist if one of the latter might be available, and he had no idea what I was talking about! Only machine-requiring chemical studies could be sent out to the central laboratory. Needless to say, this garden spot could have used a super-duper potpourri.

Though only a few steps across Madison Avenue, for the medical student it was a two-year journey from a world of classrooms to a land of hands-on training. There were few restrictions on what students could do in those days, and John Gaston was a wonderful place to get frontline experience.

During medical school one of my classmates worked in the Johnnie G. blood bank with no prior experience or training. He soon was not only drawing blood, but doing type-and-cross matches, Coombs tests, etc. It wasn't long before he was allowed to run the blood bank alone at night and on the weekends—still with no formal training or credentials. So, believe me, once the medical student made that "across the street" pilgrimage and received the short white clinical jacket, these "minor-docs" were extremely well utilized. Experience, raw and practical, was the name of the game.

Every one had their lord and master. For the students, we interns on service were the taskmasters. Actually, we could never have managed without them. Over us were the residents on service. A resident is a post-internship physician undergoing training in a particular specialty. The number or years required to complete the training depends on the particular specialty. In the pecking order the chief resident on any service is a minor deity, subservient only to a major deity, a staff physician.

The whole picture was reminiscent of a military outfit, with the staff physicians representing the generals, the residents the officers, the interns the noncoms, and the students the dogfaces. The mission—trying to deter a superior force of illness and disease that was being constantly reinforced by poverty and ignorance. Thus, the urgent need for hospitals like John Gaston—forts in the wilderness. These charity facilities, in turn, provided succulent training grounds for a variety of sorely needed medical personnel—sometimes a bit too "succulent."

Which brings us to another very important member of the team, the nurse. Typically, there was a head nurse, a graduate, in charge of either the male or female wards. Most often she—I don't recall any male nurses in those days—worked the seven A.M. to three P.M. shift, leaving in charge over the next two shifts a more senior nursing student. Like the clinical medical students, the nursing students had, shall I say, ample opportunity for hands-on experience. The nursing school had both three-and-four-year curriculums, the longer leading to a Bachelor of Science degree. Like the medical students, during their latter clinical years they rotated from one service to another. They performed all nursing duties except starting intravenous fluids, this task being left to the clinical medical students and interns, and the mundane housekeeping chores of the practical nurse and maid.

The introduction of intravenous fluid, in my opinion, has always been more an art than a science. I personally have always hated it. Today, we have these fancy "butterfly" intravenous starter needles that help a lot, but I still think a lot of the "science" is luck. Back in those days, all you had was a syringe with a needle on it—and not one of these tiny delicate things, but a *needle*. So, you felt for a vein, stuck at it through the skin with the needle-tipped syringe, all the time maintaining negative pressure by pulling back on the syringe plunger, and prayed for blood to appear.

Then, alas, the vein would roll and you'd miss it, all while the patient was groaning in agony. Reattempt. Go through the vein, bleed under the skin, try again, finally get in a vein and attach the intravenous fluid tube to the needle, only to have the fluid not flow properly. Try to adjust the angle of the in-place needle with padding and tape, or by using gravity as an ally by lowering and raising the then-used glass bottle of fluid, all in, excuse the pun, "vein." Finally, frustrated, all participants drenched in sweat, you surrender and call for help from one of your comrades. Your replacement, of course, hits the target on the first try like Robin Hood. Don't fret;

the tables will be turned tomorrow. I still hate it. Believe me, my "students" started a lot of IVs.

Although 4 percent of the total patient population was "private," there were no private rooms except for patients requiring isolation, and these were interior-decorating-wise woefully bare. All private admissions had to pay a $100 deposit unless they had insurance, a rare happenstance.

Sometimes a "V.I.P." might occupy one of these "isolation" rooms, like George, my fellow intern. He was hospitalized for several days while recovering from serum sickness after a penicillin injection—rash, swollen joints and all. I'm not sure which I thought would be worse, the sickness or the incarceration—I guess the sickness, by a hair. As it turned out, well, we'll see.

George had remained a grizzled bachelor, complete with a chiseled, non-smiling face topped with thick black hair, which he parted down the middle. While typically non-assertive, one look at those hard, muscular arms sticking out from his shirt quickly told you that this was one gent not to be toyed with. Here in the hospital his relieving medicines and meals were delivered bedside, linens were changed regularly by someone else, and he had frequent visitors bearing gifts. Though hardly the presidential suite, for him, it beat his lonely bachelor pad by a bunch.

The *coup de grace*, however, was the principal tender loving care provider, a sweet, young student nurse from Olive Branch, Mississippi. Molly

Gillman was in her early twenties, a natural blond, peaches-and-cream complexion, and had the proper proportions of everything in the right places. When you combined the heat of the season, fever from the illness, and the emotions of the moment, one can readily understand the patient's need for frequent sponge baths. It took the chief of Medicine to get George back to work! But all was not lost—Molly would likely be rotating with us the rest of the year. More to come.

Though I can't speak for the ladies, for a guy I thought being married during medical school was a distinct advantage. You had a home, complete with loving companionship and edible food, allowing a better environment for study. The poor single male had to scrounge on his own for both, allowing less time and energy for educational pursuits. During internship, the opposite was true. You were seldom home, and when you were you were either rotten company or unconscious. If a marriage could survive internship, its chances for prolonged survival were pretty good.

As before stated, the usual rotation for the intern was every third night. By that I mean a full day and night followed by another full day The next night, an off night, typically consisted of making it through the home door to the closest piece of furniture that would support your weight. Then, another full day on. The third night you became reacquainted with family, or whomever, only to start all over the next morning.

When you had the all-night duty, you were responsible for approximately one-half the entire medical service, not just your daytime ward. Even though there was an on-call bed available, with the constant calls for medications, intravenous infiltrations, or slightly deranged wandering patients, complete with wailing and dangling catheters, you seldom made its acquaintance. Many's the night the chloral hydrate and orange juice sedative cocktails flowed like wine—for the patients, not for you.

One of my fellow classmates who started his internship in January 1955 tells a hairy story of being left alone during his first month on the program for a few days after the holidays without medical students or residents. Just he and a ward full of patients. The staff physician did make daily rounds, for which he thanked the Almighty. He states he was not only overwhelmed, but also terrified. "It had to be one of the most horrible experiences of my life!" Fortunately, he survived, as did the patients.

The variety of patient ills were legend—advanced diabetics, cardiac problems, kidney disorders, all types of infectious diseases, blood dyscrasias, gastrointestinal maladies, etc. I can clearly recall a case of advanced facial blastomycosis that haunts me yet.

Staff rounds were the highlight of the day. The staff physician proceeded from bed to bed, accompanied by the nurse on duty with her rack of charts, a resident or so, the intern, and assigned students. The residents acted very wise, the intern observant, and the students eager. From bed to bed the game was repeated—differential diagnosis, tests, treatment? It was, and probably still is, a tradition enjoyed by all of the entourage, perhaps with the exception of the patient. Many of the veteran subjects, however, enthusiastically joined in the game, taking apparent pride in their obscure disorder while dropping hints to the students.

It was just at the end of our Medicine rotation when everything went sour for Mike. He had endured an unusually difficult 32-hour tour on duty, when Barbara called. She apparently was having some difficulty with the pregnancy. Mike frantically rushed home, found nothing of an emergency nature, and called their obstetrician. There apparently was nothing to do that night, so she reported to his office the next morning. Mike went on to work while waiting for a report. Much to their distress, they were told that for unknown reasons the fetus had not survived in the womb, and a missed abortion, a form of late miscarriage, was the pregnancy's fate. Barbara was fine, and though easier to take than a viable baby's death, Mike was hard hit.

At that most unfortunate time a young smart-aleck white male patient, figuring short-statured Mike an easy patsy, started giving him a hard time. It was a bad choice. He made the mistake of pushing Mike on the shoulder, and Mike responded instinctively with a swift slap to the face. Today, such a clash would have probably escalated into an "international" incident, but not then. Cooler heads prevailed, and all returned to normal—well, almost. It is rumored some reporter got wind of the incident, and the event inspired a series of critical articles concerning John Gaston in the local *Commercial Appeal* newspaper. Actually, the end results of it all were a Godsend. We'll follow up on this later.

Now, let's take an imaginary journey back to 1955 that begins, say, in the outpatient medical clinic, or, perhaps, the emergency room, where an intern decrees admission to the medical service. The enchanted trip is invariably initiated by the magic phrase, "follow the green line," which was a line painted on the floor that led through the corridors to admitting. There was also a red line to X-ray, and a yellow one to, I can't remember, maybe Oz. From there you are wheeled by some conveyance to your assigned bed. Soon your "doctor," a medical student supervised by the intern on duty, takes a detailed history, all diligently recorded, and performs a through physical examination. Specimens are then taken by the same doctor for admitting laboratory studies. Depending on the acuteness of the problem, the next to attend will be the resident, and, probably at rounds, the staff physician. Hopefully, in the not-too-distant future, you will be dismissed in much better condition than when you arrived. Unfortunately, not all did. The occasional empty bed that wasn't empty yesterday gave evidence of this sad fact of hospital life.

By the end of the three-month medical experience we truly were beginning to feel like veteran doctors, and for good reason. One might even detect a little swagger in the walk. Whether by accident or design, the next two months changed that swagger to a shuffle. Welcome to Obstetrics and Gynecology!

CHAPTER FOUR

Obstetrics and Gynecology

The name of the service may have been "Obstetrics and Gynecology," but for the intern the service was primarily Obstetrics—period. The Gynecology part was more the resident's responsibility, maybe with a little instruction of the interns on the side.

One of my old intern buddies says we spent only six weeks on this service and on Pediatrics instead of two months each, with the extra four weeks on Surgery, but I don't think so—and without official documents to the contrary, I'm doing the typing!

We, and our ever-present medical student charges, were the baby catchers—and we caught a lot of them. Including my student days, I delivered well over two hundred babies. Three of my more memorable included one in a cab outside of the hospital entrance, and two in an elevator—no, not twins. A contributing factor to the elevator births could be that we had only two elevators to, shall we say, deliver the deliveries. Suffice to say, there's a lot of mid-forty-year-old William King Smiths, or Jones, etc., running around Memphis now.

I could swear that when I went on the "OB" service that I just moved out of my apartment and into the hospital for two months. In truth, it was a twelve-hour on, twelve-hour off rotation. I guess I just don't remember ever coming home.

Rest was precious. You grabbed it whenever and wherever you could. The most frequent variety was the quick catnap on an empty gurney in the hall, which at our age, was surprisingly refreshing.

I remember one incident that well illustrates our frequent level of fatigue. It occurred after a particularly harrowing shift. I finally got the chance to doze off on a bunk bed in the on-call room, when a full-of-piss-and-vinegar comrade burst into the room laughing and yelling and generally raising hell. I snapped! I jumped up, grabbed him by his shirt and threw him across the room into the metal lockers, with every intent to do him bodily harm—I was bigger than he was, you see. Fortunately, following a rapid apology from him, complete with appropriate cower, my sanity returned.

A farcical situation occasionally occurred during my stint on obstetrics. Immediately east of the obstetric hospital was Russwood Park, the home of the Memphis Chickasaw baseball team. The on-call room I spoke of earlier was located in the rear of the building on the top floor, and was the only place you could see over the fence into the ballpark. Now, my tour on this service was precisely in the middle of summer and, thus, the baseball season. With no air conditioning, the windows had to stay open. So, if you were a big baseball fan and wanted for free to see the Chicks play, for however long you could stay—swell. But, if rest was what you had in mind, it was back to the gurneys.

Why all this fatigue? Let's go back and review the primary mission of this service, delivering babies. Essentially, the student nurses, medical students, and interns accomplished this function. The residents got into the act only if some problem arose requiring greater expertise, an infrequent but occasional occurrence.

A patient was immediately categorized when they were wheeled out of the elevator as one of two varieties, a "round one," or a "flat-top." These rather descriptive terms, which were loudly announced to all within earshot on the patients' arrival, referred to the shape of the abdomen when prone on the stretcher. If flat, not in labor and no imminent delivery, probably an "a-b." If round, a soon-to-be mother.

The "a-b" abbreviation is for the medical term "abortion." Since purposeful abortions were then against the law, the great majority were merely nature's way of terminating a bad pregnancy, better known to the public as a "miscarriage." These, in most instances, were easily handled with much less stress on the staff than an imminent birth, so often their arrival was accompanied by sighs of relief.

The "round" patient was taken directly into a labor cubicle where a student nurse took over. A medical student was assigned by the intern to sit with the patient throughout labor and record in detail its progress. The eventual delivery was accomplished either by the intern or, under his supervision, by the medical student.

The use of narcotics for relief of labor pains was stringently avoided except under unusual circumstances. I remember the patients being provided a handheld canister of some kind of gas, something similar to trichlorethylene, with an attached mask. Pressing a small button activated the canister. When the patient got a little drowsy from the sniffs, the grip on the canister became loose and the button released, with resultant prompt discontinuance of the self-administration. Actually, pretty clever.

Most of the patients were multiparous, that is, a veteran of previous births, and birthing was quick and easy. The attending medical student performed most of these deliveries. The more difficult primiparous births, first-timers who frequently required an episiotomy or forceps delivery, would be accomplished by the intern or, perhaps, a more experienced medical student under close supervision.

One of my classmates tells a story about a patient whom, as a student, he observed through a rather long and difficult labor, only to pass her on to another student at the end of his shift. Five minutes after he left the lady had a monster contraction and promptly delivered in the middle of the bed. And, to boot, the substitute got a major chewing-out. My classmate says he doesn't believe his buddy has yet forgiven him.

Picture, if you can, this scenario. New patients being wheeled down the hall, multiple labor rooms occupied, and a number of deliveries in process, all at the same time. What fun. Such a bedlam was commonplace. Yes, rest was precious.

Baby catching comes easy to some, and not so easy to others. The first thing to teach the neophyte is the proper way to receive the baby from the birth canal without dropping it. Oh, it happens. You talk about a greased pig. It's slippery. I saw a couple of babies rescued quickly from the bucket immediately below, much to the relief but embarrassment of all concerned. It helped if the student had been a football player—American football, that is—especially a halfback. The trick is in knowing the proper technique of receiving a handoff, mother to catcher, much like quarterback to halfback. A right-handed receiver will cradle the head of the baby and secure the neck in the "v" between the second and third fingers of the left hand, while using the right hand to catch the torso and direct it over the left forearm and up against the body, like a correctly carried football. This leaves the right hand free to stiff-arm, or accomplish whatever task required. With the precious bundle so secured, the dreaded "fumble" is diligently avoided.

Once the adequacy of the baby's respiration is assured, it is placed on the most convenient place possible, the now-flat abdomen of the mother, under the ever-watchful eye of the attending nurse, probably a student. The catcher in charge then takes care of the next chore, tying off and cutting the umbilical cord. Once accomplished, the baby is swept away into the loving care of the nurse for cleaning and keeping warm and comfy. The in-charge "doc" then proceeds with the clean-up chores of afterbirth disposal and repair of any episiotomy incisions or lacerations that may have occurred. Time for the champagne, or quite likely, an adjoining delivery room for same song, next verse.

For the uninitiated, an episiotomy is a loosening incision to enlarge the birth canal when it is too tight. Required, a loosening diagonal scissor cut to allow the head to pass through too tight of an opening. While sounding dreadful, it certainly is neater and more merciful than any alternative probable trauma to mother or child. While the repair that follows might not qualify as a plastic masterpiece, the results most often are very satisfactory. The human body's healing abilities are truly remarkable.

Contrary to popular opinion, the use of forceps for a delivery is not similar to removal of a cork from a wine bottle. Sometimes, when the contractions for one reason or the other can't get the job done, the use of forceps will obviate the need for an episiotomy. The trick is applying the forceps in a gentle manner so as to do no harm. This is done with a sliding, rotating maneuver that, like so many other things in life, seems to become more natural in the doing than in the explaining. Once in place, they are grasped like a post-hole digger, with the forearms parallel and the elbows close together against the abdomen of the delivering doctor. The wrists are then gently but firmly pulled out and up so as to bring the baby's head out and somewhat forward, like an affirmative nod. A piece of cake.

We usually didn't have the advantages of prenatal examinations, x-rays, sonograms and such, so you had to just play the cards you were dealt. Every now and then you got a little surprise, like a multiple birth, a breach, or some other gosh-awful presentation. Internal version and traction maneuvers are not for the timid—that's where you put on a glove up to your elbow, reach up there and try to turn the baby around so it comes out in the right position, that is, head first. Such a patient, to boot, often showed up in the late stages of labor. Surprise! What to do? Call for a resident, and the best you can.

I specifically recall such an incident when a "primip," a first-timer, came rushing in about to deliver. The nurses and I rapidly got her into a delivery room and, lo and behold, I was presented with a most fearful sight, a foot! I quickly called for the resident, who was on another floor taking care of a gynecological problem, and did the best I could while awaiting his arrival. Then, the last thing I wanted to see, I saw! The umbilical cord had fallen down around the partially exposed leg. I had visions of the cord wrapped around the baby's neck, so I tried desperately to replace it and hold off further deliverance until the resident arrived—which he did. I believe it was then and there that I decided this specialty was not for me.

I'm in no way knocking our residents. They were an amazing group. There was just a lot to do, and they could only be in one place at a time.

For example—one of the more frightening things about living in the South in those days was the ever-present danger of contracting poliomyelitis. Being before the public release of the Salk vaccine, it was just a toss of the dice. In the summer the polio wards of the nearby Infectious Disease Hospital were filled to capacity. While I was on the Obstetrics service, an emergency call came from the Infectious Disease Hospital. The call concerned a last-trimester pregnant polio patient in an iron lung who had taken a sudden turn for the worse and was dying. The chief resident immediately ran across the parking lot that separated the two buildings, performed an on-the-spot cesarean section, and unbelievably saved the baby's life. Truth, indeed, is often more amazing than fiction.

Though the drug scene was almost unheard of at that time, it did exist. One of my fellow interns tells a touching tale about an unusually handsome illegitimately pregnant black lady who, when he was on the medical service a couple of months earlier, was admitted with an acute overdose of something or other. She had required an emergency tracheotomy, that is, the insertion of a tube into her windpipe, to maintain forced breathing. He spent the night at her bedside administering every fifteen minutes injections of Picrotoxin, one of the few medications we had available at that time to counter the ill effects of the poisonous drug. Just before leaving the obstetrical service, he was called in by a resident who was in the middle of a difficult "primip" delivery, and asked to help with the anesthesia. Shortly after joining in, he noticed the tracheotomy scar, and recognized "his" Picrotoxin lady as the young mother on the table. Mother and baby did well. Obviously, a very gratifying experience for my then young fellow physician, evidenced by his still relating the story now some fifty years later.

In our "spare time" we managed a little Gynecology exposure—fibroids, cervical and uterine cancers, etc., and all the pelvic inflammatory disease you could stomach. At that time gonococcus and other venereal infections were rampant, especially among our patient population. Trichomonas infections were regarded more of a nuisance than a menace.

One of the residents was a tall, six-foot-six, rawboned type, friendly and outgoing. I recall him stuffing one of the surgical nurses in a laundry basket like she was a rag doll—all in fun, of course. During a "Gyn" teaching session, he was illustrating the art of a vaginal examination, the second and third gloved fingers of his right hand in the vagina of this amazingly cooperative patient, while the fingers of the left hand was pressing against her lower abdomen. He was exclaiming how he could easily feel between the fingers of the two hands a prominent ovarian cyst. Well, one student after the other tried, as I did, with little success, much to his disgust. I thought to myself, "With the length of those fingers he's probably feeling her tonsils instead of an ovarian cyst." Or, maybe, I just had no talent—another consideration.

As for gynecological surgery, we interns had our full of flat-top "D and Cs," that is, cervical dilatations and uterine curettements. Partial abortions, of course, are not the only indication for this procedure. The cervix of the uterus is gently dilated with insertions of graduated larger and larger probes until the required curettes can be introduced into the uterus. The inner surface of the uterus is then scraped clean. The object is to do a thorough job without perforating the uterus—a definite "no-no."

As for hysterectomies and such, this was primarily the residents' world. Our participation was largely limited to observation, unless it was your lucky day—and there were such days.

Before you knew it, the two months passed, seemingly as fast as a catnap on a gurney. But, before leaving, we were asked by the staff to do a reprise of an "OB" skit I had written earlier for a medical class party.

Before high school football became my everything, momma assured I got in a few years of classical piano. Of course, during high school my three Bs changed from Bach, Beethoven and Brahms to Boogie, Blues and Broadway. While at Duke, I wrote music for original student musical comedies. So, take-off parodies were my meat. For this one, *South Pacific* was the victim.

Mike, with his deceiving baby face and shorter stature, had good-naturedly agreed to play the innocent mother in the original medical school skit. Despite Barbara's recent tragedy, he said he would do it here again for the staff. I took the part of the attending doctor.

In way of a sampling—a "primip's" opening soliloquy. "What is this I feel, can it be a baby, won't somebody save me, whatever can I do?" To which the doctor replies, "Belly high it could be, belly high 'tis true—an examination would do just to see, you agree—belly high, belly high, belly high!" Then after a very cursory exam, the doctor exclaims, "Some enchanted evening you will have a stranger, you will have a stranger off in a crowded room, and somehow you'll know, you'll know even then, that some day you'll feed it again and again!" Pre-delivery, of course, there's the prepping song, "We're going to wash those germs right out of her hair." And, finally, the big ending, the new mother proudly presenting her "eleven and one pounds of fun, here's my little honey-bun, and every pound was packed with dynamite," with appropriate rolling of the eyes.

A short finale to an exhausting but very rewarding service. No time for prolonged farewells. Duty called. Duty always was calling on Obstetrics and Gynecology.

We returned to what we had previously thought was a horribly grueling one-night-on-two-nights-off schedule—now, heaven! And the new patients? A direct continuation, Pediatrics.

John Gaston

Theresa Gaston Mann

Gaston Hotel (on the right), Court Square

Memphis General Hospital, opened in 1898

John Gaston Hospital, opened in 1936

JOHN GASTON HOSPITAL

John Gaston Hospital, aerial view

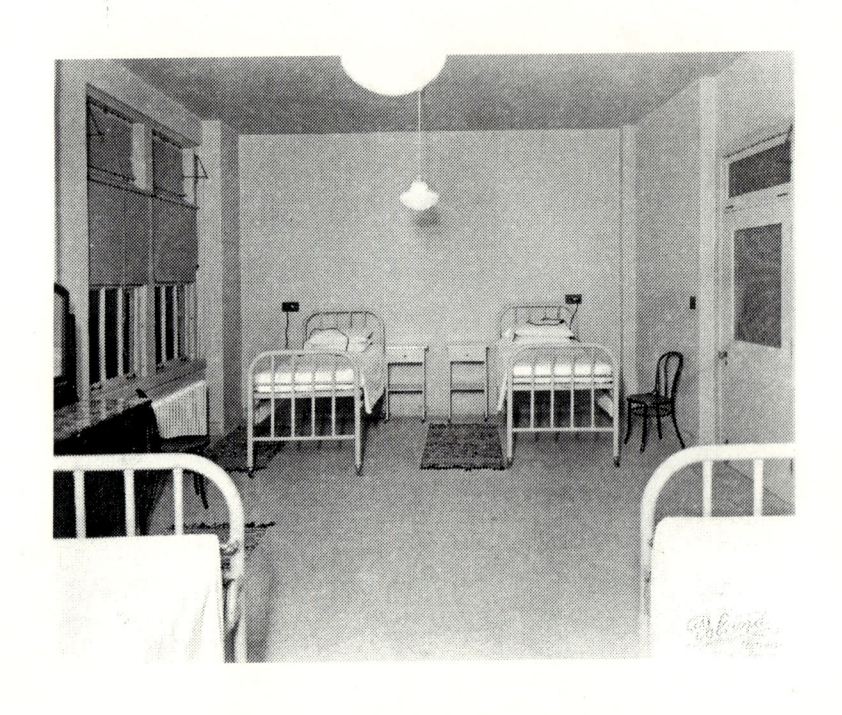

Patient room, maternity ward

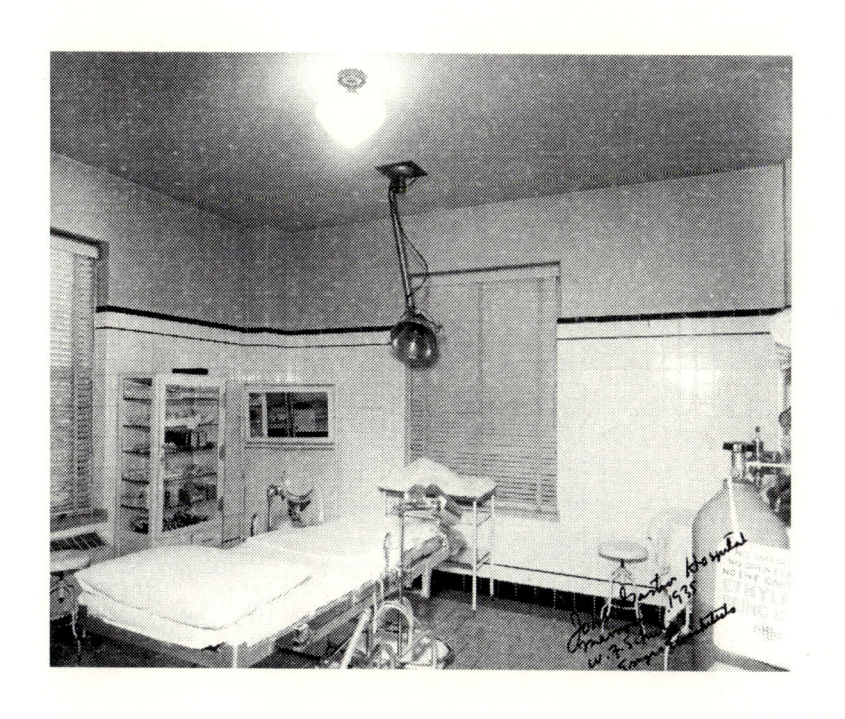

Operating room, minor

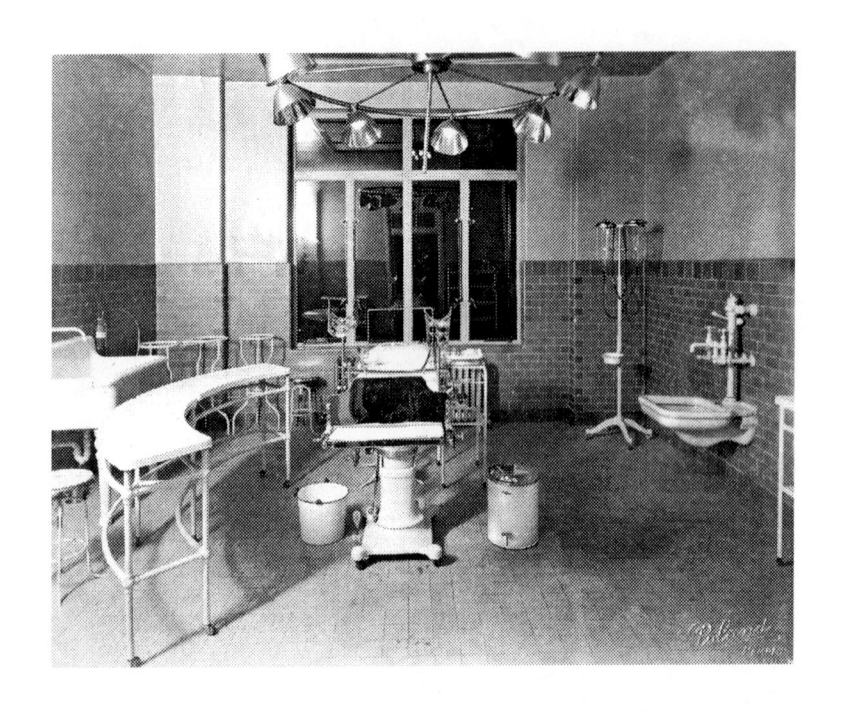

Operating room, major

Doctor's and intern's lounge

CHAPTER FIVE

Pediatrics

The pediatric wards were in the Frank Tobey building located behind the main hospital, It was connected to the latter by a long first-floor corridor, similar to the one connecting the maternity suites on the east side.

The sounds and smells were essentially the same as those in any pediatric hospital, except, because of the open wards and lack of artificial cooling, probably more intense than most. On the first floor to the right was a room full of iron lungs, evidencing the constant presence of the infantile paralysis threat. There was also a number of smaller patient rooms on the floor that contained various machines, pumps, and other apparatus required for special nursing care. The wards above were pretty much a repeat of the medical service arrangement.

In addition to inpatient ward care, the outpatient clinics, day and night, had to be manned. With only six interns on service, we had plenty to do. For the inpatients, admission history and physical examinations, laboratory work, student assignment, staff rounds, etc., were essentially the same as on the medical service, and by now familiar. The main difference was the patients, kids—from the very young to the teens. Frightened, brave, lonely, and sometimes amazingly cheerful kids.

And, while many of the illnesses were the same as on the adult wards, there were those that seemed reserved for these younger innocents. Nephrotic syndrome, whooping cough, rheumatic fever, meningitis, and post-viral measles/mumps/chicken pox encephalitides come immediately to mind. Hydrocephalic children with their balloon-shaped heads were especially heart-wrenching, there being no shunting surgery performed at that time to relieve the problem. Also present, the multiple varieties of other congenital deformities that again presented more surgical challenge than present expertise could successfully manage.

Sickle cell anemia is a congenital disorder of the red blood cells that is primarily confined to the Negro race. As such, it was very common in our young patient population. It often presents initially as a terribly painful "crisis" from inadvertent blood clotting. Eventually, it can destroy the spleen, with resulting fatal complications. Still today there is no cure.

All the childhood leukemias and lymphomas you hear of today were also with us, but, other than steroids, none of the current medications were yet developed. Prognosis was dismal.

The two most common problems, as now, were the pneumonias and the gastrointestinal infections. The pneumonias most frequently followed an influenza or other viral respiratory outbreak, while poor sanitation largely contributed to the latter. Fortunately, we had at that time sulfur, penicillin, cloromycetin, streptomycin, and two of the new tetracyclines, aureomycin and terramycin, with which to work. God sends.

Dehydration, especially with the gastrointestinal disorders, was a frequent problem that had to be dealt with, one way or the other. Intravenous infusion was always the first choice. On the younger patients a scalp vein was often utilized. Or, if all else failed, instead of surgically exposing a vein, the required fluid could be infused subcutaneously, that is, in the soft tissue under the skin. From here the fluid is slowly absorbed. Like on the medical wards, these tasks were the intern's and his assigned medical students' responsibility.

As again was collection of urine, blood, cerebrospinal fluid, or whatever for laboratory studies—just as on the medical wards. With strap-on devices of one kind or the other, urine collection was seldom a problem. Not so for the other two. Especially, from the younger children with meager veins and no hope of co-operation, one usually had to collect blood from a larger and deeper vessel. Most commonly chosen was the major vein from the leg, the femoral, that runs in the groin parallel to the major femoral artery and nerve to the leg. From medial to lateral they run vein, artery, nerve,—V.A.N. So, the pulsating artery is palpated, and a rather long needle is inserted just medially, while pulling back on the syringe plunger. If you happened to get arterial blood, deeper red and pulsating, it wasn't a disaster—a little pressure and the bleeding usual stopped promptly. But, you didn't want to hit the nerve. Or was it N.A.V.? Just kidding!

The lumbar tap for cerebrospinal fluid was initially somewhat nerve wracking, but after getting the feel of gentle insertion, allowing the fluid to freely drip through the special needle into the waiting test tube, it soon became less fearful. All in a day's work.

This brings up a remembrance close to my heart. Though not a true part of the John Gaston story, my beloved baby daughter, still in her infancy, was suddenly afflicted with a non-relenting diarrhea. I consulted a local pediatrician who admitted her to Le Bonheur Children's Hospital, a private prestigious pediatric hospital located directly behind the University of Tennessee medical complex. All diagnostic tests were non-revealing, yet the problem persisted. She was sustained with scalp IVs, but no essential improvement occurred. With my personal allergy history, I suggested a possible allergic etiology, cause, that is, but with no telltale eosinophil allergy cells seen in the microscopic examination of the stools, this suggestion was ignored. Finally, suspecting sprue, a rare intestinal disorder, they placed her on a "banana diet," a food that sprue patients tolerate. She immediately responded favorably. It was later after numerous food feeding trials we deduced she didn't have sprue, but rather a milk allergy. For years after, she could not have a piece of cake made with milk without developing asthma. Undoubtedly, this experience was one of the prime motivating factors for my later allergy endeavors.

Speaking of Le Bonheur, our pediatric residents rotated over there for a more full-rounded program. One of them I got to know fairly well during our misadventures there. He was, shall I say, a "very healthy" Aussie—you know, a light-complexioned, ruggedly handsome type. One of our head pediatric nurses was a buxom, attractive thirty-some-year-old. Although I do recall a few varicose veins, she also was "very healthy"—nobody's perfect. All of a sudden he was gone, back to Australia, and so was our nurse. Ain't love grand.

There wasn't a lot of joviality on the pediatric tour, but I do remember the day Mike and I were joking around in the hall on the second floor, you know, a little good-natured roughhousing, when we sort of bumped into a large oxygen tank. It toppled over with a loud clang, and the gage apparatus broke off. Suddenly, the headless beast took off straight down the hall. It looked like a torpedo in one of those World War II movies! Had he been there, our submariner, George, would have been homesick. Fortunately, no one was hurt, so Mike and I did a quick disappearing act. What oxygen tank?

The nights on pediatric ward duty were also much the same as on the medical service—the differences, as would be expected, predicated by the patients' age difference. A lot more crying, a lot less wailing. The need of personal and frequent night inspection was far greater, especially of the younger children, because they more often could not tell you the cause of their distress. It may be nothing more than a cry for attention or for the disposal of a soiled diaper, but it could be the heralding of a true medical emergency. Thus, the nickname of the service, "veterinary medicine." The "on" nights, indeed, were more often truly "on," and rest was a rarity.

The required two months were a blur and passed before you knew it. In retrospect, they were invaluable. However, unless you had a true passion for cutting, the next two months were, in essence, slave labor—with an occasional bone thrown your way. Relief from boredom was possible if you could master one trick, and most of us did, sleeping with your eyes open. You'll see what I mean. On to General Surgery.

CHAPTER SIX

General Surgery

Like Gynecology, General Surgery was a "residents" service. We interns were the "assistants," in other words, retractor holders and knot tiers. I guess I was more critical at the time because, during my off quarter halfway through medical school, I had worked at the Baptist, a private hospital down the street, doing nothing but assisting private practice surgeons. I scrubbed so much my hands and arms were literally raw! I had "been there, done that" and didn't need or want to do that for another two months.

Admittedly, it was an essential exposure for those without such previous experience. Just knowing how to hold a scalpel, scissors or forceps is a learned, not a natural skill. But "OB" service had already provided, in my then opinion, ample opportunity for that. I supposed knot-tying technique could be polished a bit, and needlework repair techniques improved. After all, emergency room trauma patients were just around the corner. Little did I know.

Of course, the outpatient clinic was always with

us. Though the actual schedule now escapes me, the lesser care and smaller surgical needs, such as dressing changing and boil lancing, were taken care of by the students or we interns. Major diagnosis and yes-or-no surgical decisions were the residents' responsibility.

For those who craved surgery and nothing else, those natural-born cutters, they took to this service like a duck to water. And, sometimes their enthusiasm was rewarded if you were working with a "nice-guy" resident. You might get to perform some of an operation, or "close," that is, sew up the incision. I remember one of my classmates, a later thoracic surgeon, bragging about how he was allowed to do a chest case "skin to skin," that is, incision through sewing up—if true, a rare occurrence.

But, especially when a staff surgeon was involved, you were usually third down on the totem pole—strictly relegated to the Daever retractor. The shouts today still ring loud and clear, "Don't just lean back on the Daever, retract, retract!" This is where the previously mentioned trick, "sleeping with your eyes open," came in handy.

J.J., you remember, the lone female intern, related to me a story about being assigned on a very busy evening to assist a particularly obnoxious staff surgeon. On discovering she was to be his only helper, he raised holy hell, if there is such a thing, proclaiming loudly that he didn't want to operate with any female anytime, anywhere, anyhow! Unfortunately, or, depending on your point of view, fortunately, no one else was available. He was stuck with this female intern. Jennifer says she was really feeling bad that night and thought at one point she might faint, but after his rantings there was no way short of a heart attack they could get her out of that room. You had to know J.J. to fully appreciate the electricity in the air that night.

You might think with surgery being more a scheduled event, the one-night-out-of-three rotation would allow ample time for rest and relaxation. After all, the "on-call" staff room was handy, being located on the sixth floor right next to the surgical suites. Well, think again. In addition to the routine surgical emergencies, you know acute appendicitis, bleeding gastric ulcers, intestinal obstructions etc., remember this was the trauma hospital for the city. Along with the usual auto accidents, et al, man's inhumanity to man was most apparent in the middle of the night. In the 'fifties the knife seemed the weapon of choice, though guns, clubs and brickbats also took their toll.

Actually, a break in the action did infrequently occur during the evening shifts, during which the surgical nursing staff might, shall I say, become inclined to be a tad lackadaisical. To assure that the city was getting its just due, the two night shift nursing supervisors would make unannounced visits—hell bent for leather. Amazingly, each visit invariably found the staff industriously keeping the surgical suites shipshape. What the "supers" didn't know was that they had a traitor in their midst! Seems that the nurses had befriended the little old night shift switchboard operator whose office was directly across from the elevators. When he saw them get on an elevator he would give the nurses a quick buzz and warn them that, as he called them, the old "biddies" were on the way. It pays to have friends in high places.

I've been asked how we handled homosexuality on the staff. The answer, we didn't. In the 'fifties in the South, homosexuality was a closet thing. Unlike today where in many places it is an accepted alternate lifestyle, it was then and there strictly taboo. So, while it unquestionably did exist, most were not aware of it.

The only instance I can recall that aroused my suspicion occurred early during my rotation on this service. I was earnestly engaged in holding my retractor as third man on the totem pole when a surgical resident came up behind me and proceeded to watch the case over my shoulder. It was a rather long, complicated abdominal case of some interest, so this was a usual occurrence. Suddenly, to my surprise, his presence, especially his hips, became more than near. In fact, as Groucho Marx once said, if he were any closer he would have been in front of me! With the staff surgeon and other residents there, I didn't want to cause a disturbance, nor did I want to delay the case by breaking scrub—by that I mean touching a non-sterile area and having to cease retracting to change my gown and gloves. So, I did the only thing I could think to do, I stepped firmly on his toe. I guess he got the idea because he promptly disappeared. Since nothing was said or occurred thereafter, I still don't yet know whether I was being molested or initiated.

The surgical patient wards were on the two floors directly beneath the surgical suites. The bed arrangements, labs and all were similar to those on the medical wards. Medical staffing, student and nursing responsibilities were essentially the same. The General Surgery patients were located usually on the fourth floor, while the Orthopedic, Urology, and other surgical specialty patients were on the fifth floor. Rotations were the same. Crowded conditions were the same.

The summer heat discomfort was also the same, and similarly handled—open windows and ceiling fans. The one major difference was the divers. Being higher, an occasional despondent patient, despite protective screening, would attempt to jump! Some succeeded, some didn't.

On a more joyful note, George and Molly were again on the same service. I'm telling you it was sickening. They were frequently seen, as a gossip columnist would say, in a romantic corner of the hospital cafeteria at all hours, "partaking of a sumptuous repast." The cafeteria served five meals a day, the usual three plus complete meals at eleven P.M. and three A.M. It's a wonder George didn't weigh 300 pounds. Oh well, I don't guess gluttony was George's main motivation. Now, if they could pull that off, you know their heads were in the clouds.

George had managed to save a few nickels from his navy days and, on the rare occasion of a mutual night off, would take his lady love to Pappy and Jimmy's Lobster Shack, his favorite Memphis eatery. George was well known as a fervent penny squeezer, so this had to be getting serious.

There appears to be two primary personality types in Medicine, the impatient, demonstrative extrovert and the patient, timid introvert. A cut-'em-up bull surgeon versus a Casper-milk-toast internist comes to mind. All other varieties are blends, each specialty perhaps better served by a particular "special" mixture. I was still trying to pinpoint my blend, and time was running out.

By the end of my surgery rotation I did realize one thing for sure. I did not have the guts to be a general practitioner. A specialist with the required advanced training had expertise in at least something. Becoming a specialist, however, took more work, more time, and more family sacrifice, but it was for the rest of your life. There had to be a way.

In retrospect, regardless of my bellyaching, my time in General Surgery did help, not just in honing my surgical skills, but in comprehension between the ears. I obviously liked surgery or I would not have spent my off-quarter of medical school doing surgery full-time. Also, in addition to my two months in a surgical rotation during internship, I later spent the four months I had to wait before reporting to Uncle Sam working as an assisting doctor in a private General Surgery clinic. No question, surgery was somewhat in my bones, but not as much as it was in those of the "real" surgeons'. My "blend" apparently needed more person-to-person contact than General Surgery allowed. I needed more, as it is known in the profession, patient rapport.

This search for personal "blend" satisfaction was one reason a month of the year-long rotation was left open for an "elective." There were all the surgical specialties to consider, like Urology and Orthopedics, or the various medical specialties, like Pulmonology or Dermatology. But, again I felt these programs were the domains of the resident, with the intern only a flunkie. And, at least at that time, I had no great interest in any of them. In college I had minored in Psychology, and had always been fascinated by this field. So, with Gailor Psychiatric Hospital immediately at hand, along with a craving for a month of more reasonable existence, I chose Psychiatry.

CHAPTER SEVEN

Psychiatry

Lost, I was absolutely lost when I walked into the Gailor Psychiatric Hospital. My schedule was much less hectic, much less grind, much less stress, almost too much less! In the care of both outpatients and inpatients I was primarily an observer with nothing to contribute. One of my medical school classmates had worked at Gailor during medical school as an orderly, and initially that's exactly what I felt like, an orderly. I had to adapt to this more passive involvement and, over a couple of weeks, I did just that.

The psychiatric staff physicians and residents were very generous with their knowledge, patiently explaining to me the characteristics of each diagnosis, possibly helpful treatment techniques, and probable prognosis. I soon was able to identify by observation the manic-depressives, paranoiac schizophrenics, catatonics, acute and chronic depressions, psychotics, etc.

The more violent varieties were kept in the lockup patient quarters in the basement. The non-violent were placed on the upper floors where the quarters were more open, and they could mingle in community sitting rooms. Treatment facilities. conference rooms, and staff offices were also located on the upper floors.

While some psychiatric calming drugs like thorazine were available, the choices compared to today were very limited. Though I witnessed none, the various shock techniques were sometimes utilized. Group conferences called "milieus," and occasional hypnotism were in common usage. Psychoanalysis, as we know it today, was yet on the horizon, destined to become primarily a tool for private patients in years to come. At best, available treatment modalities were generally long-range therapies with slow progress, presenting little recognizable results during my brief time on service. I have no recollection of lobotomies being performed, the operation Jack Nicholson had in the movie *One Flew Over the Cuckoo's Nest*. I don't think so.

I specifically remember being drawn to an attractive young white lady, lithe, brunette, soft-spoken, friendly. Playing psychiatrist, I talked to her at length about her childhood, her parents, her background, etc. She seemed a lot more normal than many of my everyday acquaintances. I thought for sure she would soon be ready for discharge back to her previous life. I was totally destroyed when, on discussing her case with her psychiatrist, he informed me that she was probably an incurable schizophrenic who would spend the rest of her days in such an institution. I decided then and there that I was not tough enough for this job.

The longer I was there the more demoralizing were the tasks at hand. The catatonics in their ridiculous poses, the ever-melancholic depressions, the violent psychotics, et al, were heartbreaking. No, I just wasn't tough enough. If medical treatment couldn't take care of the problem, I guess the surgeon in my "blend" wanted to just "cut it out" and be done with it—like a stomach ulcer. Couldn't be done. Thank God, literally, we have more effective tools to work with today—but there is still a long, long way to go.

But, on a happy note, I was home more often, better rested, and actually able to go out and socialize once in a while. I became reacquainted with my wife and daughter, which was very therapeutic for all concerned. We often got to go to church together on Sundays, occasionally take our little girl to the park, visit with her grandparents, etc. You know, function like a real family, if only for short intervals. I guess my "elective" month might have been more beneficial to my "psyche" than were my meager contributions to the mental health of the patients.

I remember one special evening we were invited for dinner by one of the Psychiatry residents and his wife. They were hospitable, though, shall I say, curiously "naïve." Before dinner he asked if we would care for a cocktail. I answered affirmatively, and offered to help. He eagerly accepted and we went into the kitchen. He produced an unopened half-pint of "Four Roses" bourbon, with which he had no idea what to do. I fixed very weak highballs for the two of us, none for the ladies. After dinner he suggested playing cards. I asked about bridge. He agreed, and then asked us to teach them how to play the game. Eventually he thought he got the idea, and proceeded to deal the cards. He cut the deck in half and the tried to force the two halves together. He didn't know how to shuffle cards. I shuffled the cards for him. After a few hands, because of my early-morning duty, we thanked them for a lovely evening and departed. An afterthought—how could anyone so out of touch with life's little trivialities possibly be equipped to deal with the often raw emotional needs of the psychiatrically confused? On the other hand, maybe all that stuff just gets in the way.

Mike, for his elective month, chose Ophthalmology, feeling it may be useful in his plans to become a flight surgeon in the Air Force after internship. George chose Orthopedics. This would have been my father's choice for me, he as a chiropodist being frequently associated with the local bone doctors—but that cracking and sawing stuff was not for me. I was just not the carpenter type.

George, however, had other things on his mind than bone crunching. The graduating nurses had their big dance in early December at the Silver Slipper, a local upper-level nightspot. Can't you see it, a full mid-'fifties dance band complete with male and female vocalists, dreamy danceable music, the large dance floor with a big rotating mirrored ball that made the whole place sparkle—the full Monty in those days. And Molly was beautiful with her orchid graduation corsage. The submariner was torpedoed. George, already having served his hitch in the armed services, proposed wedding bells for the spring after he established a residency in Orthopedics, and Molly accepted.

In the meantime while all the above was happening, the politicos were changing our world, albeit a little late! Oh well, better late than never. I don't know if Mike's patient slap had anything to do with it, but it's my book and I'm going to give him the credit! It began on June 19, 1955 when the first of a series of newspaper articles critical of John Gaston Hospital were published in the *Memphis Commercial Appeal* newspaper. It all came to a pleasant conclusion while I was still on the Psychiatry service, as explained December 18, 1955 in the same newspaper.

According to the articles, over several years there had been a crescendo of complaints to the Community Council from various member agencies concerning inefficiencies at John Gaston Hospital. Despite repeated promises to attend to these concerns, they complained that nothing had been improved.

In the articles there were multiple examples provided, but in essence they focused attention on four specific functions—delays in admission, lack of concern by admitting personnel, cases of personal hardship from billing practices, and lack of sufficient staffing of the emergency room, Noteworthy to us was the statement that the agencies had no complaints about treatment of patients once admission was accomplished. That let us off the hook, the complaints concerning business and not professional matters. You recall, business and professional responsibilities were administered separately, the former by the City, and the latter by the University.

After a lot of meetings, discussions, arbitrations, et al, the following changes were announced—an expansion of hours in the outpatient clinics; acquisition of additional interviewing and screening staff; individual consideration of hardship cases caused by the 50 cents clinic charge; a more efficient referral "pink slip" system from the emergency room to the various clinics; a number of physical plant structural improvements, including curtain cubicles in the wards; an increase in bed and bathroom living quarters on the sixth floor to six for interns and eight for residents; an updating of the air-conditioning in the emergency room; two interns to be on duty in the emergency room two-thirds of the day, with one on duty over the early 12 A.M. to 8 A.M. shift; an increase in the number of interns from 36 to 40, with the intention of raising the number to 48 over the next year (didn't affect us); **and, finally, a raise in**

house staff stipends from the present $35 to $75 per month, with an extra $25 for married interns and residents who maintain outside living quarters!

Yippee! We were rich! The next Saturday night I was off duty, so we had a celebratory gala in our back yard—intern style. We provided a salad, set-ups, and charcoal grill; you bring your own meat, booze and whatever. The guests? Fellow off-duty classmate interns, of which there were darned few, and old Memphis friends just finishing or having just completed their particular educational pursuit—lawyer, architect, business, etc.—with appropriate female companionship, of course. J.J. was on duty.

We were all in the same situation, lots of dreams for the future, but no cash for the present. I recall my later award-winning architect friend and his charming family living like church mice, never allowing himself to carry more than a quarter in his pocket for fear he may spend more than that daily allotment. Yea, though the social amenities were sparse, we had more than an abundance of true comradeship. The laughter was robust, the harmony was, well, we thought true. Possibly "The Road to Mandalay" might have gotten a little out of hand when my father piped in—that's when some non-appreciative neighbor asked the police to put a muffler on it! But, given the circumstances, while politely requesting moderation, the men in blue briefly joined the chorus. Some of the best times of our lives. It's hard to beat all that youth and enthusiasm.

All in all, though perhaps a bit biased, I thought the changes at John Gaston were good, especially those concerning the salary increase and the "pit," that is, the emergency room, my next and last assignment. I'm glad I got that extra rest while on Psychiatry, because I was surely going to need it shortly, as you shall see.

The month ended well, with a touch of sadness. It was very likely to be our last Christmas at home. As usual, my mother assured it was memorable, complete with a big, well-decorated tree, amply piled beneath with beautifully wrapped gifts, and, of course, toys for the granddaughter. And the food, well, her maiden name was Foppiano, and you know Italian mothers, even when they are only half-Italian. As she always said, "Turkey and lasagna naturally go together." It was indeed a merry and memorable family occasion. We were all happy, healthy, and hopeful. If we could only learn to enjoy those blessed moments more, before they change. They inevitably will, you know. Time takes its toll.

CHAPTER EIGHT

Emergency Room

As the administrator assured, there were two interns on duty two-thirds of the day, and one during the early-morning shift. Being there was only six of us on the E.R. service, that made the shift rotation rather obvious, with five of us on everyday and one off. As in most charity hospital emergency rooms, our activities were multiple and varied—all types of acute illnesses in all age groups, acute surgical emergencies, obstetrical problems requiring immediate attention, acute cardiovascular episodes, sudden neurological and mental disturbances, poisonings, etc.—and trauma! All kinds of trauma—sports, home, vehicular, accidental, intentional, etc., either to take care of on the spot or, after any necessary emergency care, triage to an appropriate treatment area.

We had enough problems trying to take care of the legitimate workload, so when "clinic" patients through misrepresentation masquerading as emergencies got in ahead of the truly needy, we got pretty "hot." Oh, I can understand their motivation—

quicker service, less red tape, etc. They were nevertheless a damnable nuisance. Where once it was near impossible to kick them out, now, with the newly installed "referral system," we had a slick way of moving them out the door. They were declared non-emergency patients, and "pink-slipped" directly to the outpatient clinic of our choice, marked for special handling "today," "tomorrow," or "as soon as possible." Bye! I liked it.

Contrary to the lyric of that old World War II song, "Saturday night is the loneliest night of the week," in the E.R. at John Gaston, it was just the opposite. On Saturday nights we were bombarded. By far, the favorite implement for settling differences amongst our primary constituents was, as previously noted, the "knife"—and there seemed to always occur an extraordinary number of differences on Saturday nights. Allow me to introduce you to the "cut" room.

Those "incisions" not severe enough to require repair under general anesthesia, the great majority, were repaired on the spot in a side room we lovingly referred to as the "cut" room. With only two, or, on the early-morning shift, one intern available in the emergency room, the resulting "suture line" didn't move very rapidly. Now and then a patient leaning against the wall would just slide down to the floor and pass out. Oh, a nurse would always jump to the rescue to obviate any catastrophe. Fortunately, we usually had volunteer help from a number of medical students who, not having anything better to do, would show up to get "sewing" experience. No, though perhaps hard to believe, no one ever bled to death, at least, not to my knowledge.

But before continuing with the E.R. story, allow me to remind my readers that, to be successful at any interpersonal endeavor, one must be able to communicate with the second party. E.R. docs are no exception—you have to be able to communicate with your patients. Special schooling in this necessary skill began for the medical students approximately three years prior when they crossed Madison Ave. and began the required course, "Afro-American Slang 101." Such bilingualism was essential if one was to obtain any semblance of an accurate history.

True, while certain folk medicine or venereal terms might have been mutually understood, otherwise so-called normal conversation would have been undecipherable without the previously mentioned training.

For an example—the police bring in a young black male to assure his fitness for jail. He presents the following story. I shall try to attempt translation as we go along.

"Trying to be a back door man [married lady's lover], and tip out [cheat on your spouse] with this hammer banana [very handsome light-skinned black lady] who, I had been told had been fruiting around [being promiscuous], I was nigh on to grand rations [making love] when my flappers [ears] pick up a knock at the door! Thinking it was her coo-you [crazy] Bigger Thomas [bad Negro] who would peel my bark [skin], put me in a tree suit [coffin] and send me to marble city [the cemetery], I moved my stompers [feet] to the Chamber of Commerce [toilet] and out the window! Waiting for me outside was the nebs [police] with headache sticks [night sticks]. We had a little gin [street fight]. Then they took me off in their screaming gasser [patrol car with siren] to this pad of stitches [hospital]. But all I got is a little red gravy [blood] under the rind [skin] of my benders [arms] and chimney [head]. I think I got a real haircut [wrongdoing from a woman]. That's the problem when your nose is wide open [being in love]. But I'm not in the dustbin yet [not dead yet]. Dig? [Comprehend?]"

Conclusion—check for head injuries, probably only a few bruises, and off to jail. (Okay, so I got a little help off the Internet from Clarence Major's *Afro-American Slang Dictionary*—it's been almost fifty years!)

Hey! Don't get me wrong. I'm in no way stereotyping. Remember, our clientele was not from the intelligentsia. Admittedly, the majority of our patients were of a more gentile nature, but those brought in by the police were usually not of that variety. And being the charity facility of the area, just like so many other such urban hospitals across the country, we were the primary caregivers to that variety of clientele, whether black or some other ethnic variety. Strictly a matter of geography at the time.

Among my medical experiences in the area, I remember meeting and associating with many black fellow citizens of the highest moral and intellectual caliber. Specifically, I recall two black nurses, the most dedicated, and inspiring professionals I can recall, along with a number of spectacular role-model teachers. But they were from another world. You get the idea.

For sure, emergency room experiences were diverse, some being comedic, others frightening, and on occasion some being better classified as "interesting."

We had no special detention rooms for prisoner patients in the hospital, though with the new improvements such were planned for the future. So, it was not unusual to see prisoners brought into the emergency room handcuffed or shackled to a gurney awaiting medical care. Somewhat awkward for all, perhaps, but expedient.

J.J. tells an amusing story on one of our classmates that she shared her tour of duty with in the E.R. This guy was a real "hunk" to the ladies, not at all boisterous or boorish, but more of a quiet, strong "Gregory Peck" type. Every week the police would haul in the same two handcuffed prostitutes who, in the spirit of the game, would feign some abdominal problem. J.J. giggles that if they found her on duty, they suddenly lost interest and quickly recovered. On the other hand, if the "hunk" was on, the problems would suddenly magnify, requiring full evaluation and examination. The gals liked to play their little games.

I encountered a similar situation. Almost like clockwork every few days the police would forcibly drag in two female prisoners, shackled, cursing and spitting. They were both Caucasian, one a blond of sorts, the other a redhead. I'm not sure what their incarcerations were for, though I could hazard a guess. To us they were simply "wrist-cutters." In their warped minds they had this thing going with the local police, a sort of razor blade "hide-and-seek." I will say this for them, they were ingenious! How they kept from slicing up their own body cavities, I'll never know. At any rate, they seemed to get a perverse pleasure from making their jailors forcibly take them out of jail to the hospital for repair of their self-inflicted wounds. Actually, they were quite skilled surgeons, as they never did any serious damage to nerves, tendons or such. After repeated such episodes, I decided to befriend rather than aggravate, and, after suturing the redhead's wrist one more time, I reminded her that I had been nice to her, and asked a favor. I told her I was going off duty in two hours, and please to wait until after then to do the other wrist. She smiled. Sure enough, as I was walking out that evening I heard the all-too-familiar dragging, spitting and cursing in the hallway ahead. As I passed by on my way out, the redhead looked up at me, silently smiled, and gave me a little wave—and I, from the heart, blew her a little kiss. I was tired.

It was during the last hour of the late shift I experienced a rather frightening encounter with a very large, hulking, middle-aged black patient. There was something odd about him, his whole attitude being rather paranoid and sinister. I realized that I was the only doctor there, and I didn't like it. Carefully questioning him, I surmised he felt someone or something was doing or about to do him grievous harm. But I couldn't get it out of him exactly what it was, or what he wanted me to do about it. He finally mumbled something about being poisoned. He suspected someone had put something in his beer. I wasn't sure he had all his oars in the water, so I was getting more and more concerned. I then noticed just outside the treatment room a couple of guys that had come in with him were chuckling. I began to get the idea. I sniffed his beer he had brought in for "analysis." They had urinated in his beer! Now, admittedly, that's not too funny, but a heck of a lot less tragic than other imagined alternatives. I snickered and told him what had happened. I made a mistake. For what seemed an eternity he sat there, silently seething. Then he slowly rose, mumbling something about killing someone. George, good old George, just then came on duty. I gave him the "hey" sign. Sensing my anxiety, he quickly sized up the situation and was able to calm down the big guy by relating a similar post-liberty prank in the navy that, while not funny, was harmless. The smoldering giant appeared somewhat appeased when George chastised the "buddies" for their bad taste, and for wasting the otherwise urgently needed time and energy of the hospital staff. I wouldn't need to be reminded to get George and Molly a special wedding gift.

I, and others of my gender, had from time to time noted the presence in the admission office of a very attractive, yes, sexy lady. She was a brunette with long curly hair that swung freely just shy of her waist as she walked. Her figure was exceptional. Being an obviously "older" woman, at least two or three years older than I, and slightly standoffish, she was categorized in my mind as a sort of an interesting background curiosity. Again, during what seems to be the witching hour just before the opening eight A.M. bell, Miss "Jones," or whatever was her name, casually stuck her head in my office and asked if I would take a quick look at her sore throat. No big deal. No formal chart or such required, just a quick look. Sure, just step in the treatment room while I get a tongue blade. When I stepped back in she untied a couple of strings and suddenly was standing there in the altogether! Oh my! Shaken to my timbers, my first response was a natural male hormonal shower. Propriety quickly replaced this reaction with a realization of the implausibility, and inappropriateness of the situation! I carefully cleared my throat, which was very dry at the time, and while draping her with a sheet, explained that the nurse was on her way out, and we would have to make her an appointment for a full examination first thing tomorrow. After checking her throat, I prescribed some lozenges, and quickly lit out for home, perhaps a little more perspiry and breathless than usual. To my relief, I think, no follow-up visit was ever made. I guess the lozenges did the trick. I suppose that experience would be classified under the "interesting" category.

There also was the mundane, the everyday chores—at least that's what they seemed to be after awhile. An example would be the constant flow of acute asthmatics. The children we turned over to the pediatric clinic folks pronto. The adults, often in severe distress, were usually treated very efficiently with a direct syringe of IV aminophylline. The fancy steroids, etc., were too slow. Truly, those IVs were miracle stuff. You just had to be careful not to overdo.

Another "mundane"—venereal disease, as before noted was very prevalent in our patient population. Other than referral to the proper service for required care, however, it was not an emergency room responsibility—with one frequent exception, stricture. Acute bladder obstruction from post-gonorrheal urethral stricture was a daily visitor. Required? Urethral stricture dilatation with gradually enlarging metal catheters. No fun for anyone, dilated or dilator! But, then, neither is acute bladder obstruction. Now, such then commonplace complications of the gonorrheal scourge have all but disappeared with the advent of effective antibiotics. With emergence of new resistant bacteria, however, some of these old horrors could again become frequent emergency room problems. Let's hope not.

Thus, in amazing short order, the unusual became routine, and the routine became mundane. Before you realized it, the two months had passed. And so had your internship.

CHAPTER 9

Epilogue

It was over. No celebration, no confetti, it was just over. Oh, I would get some sort of certificate, but that was it. It had been like an exciting trip down a road that suddenly ended at the edge of a cliff. No more road, no more journey.

It was on to the next phase of life. For me, as for most of us, there was no big decision to make; it had already been dictated, except for the direction: Army, Navy, or Air Force. Mike had chosen the Air Force where he planned to become a flight surgeon. By previous agreement he reported for duty shortly after completing the internship. I, concluding that I could walk further than I could either fly or swim, chose Army green.

It was in reality no big deal. There was no shooting war going on in the world at that time and, whichever direction you chose, you would receive over your tour of duty sustenance for you and your family. It could be a waste of time or an inconvenience, but that largely depended on the luck of the draw. So, you might as well kick back, relax and go with the flow.

I, unlike Mike, was faced with one minor problem. I would not begin my tour of duty for four months until the next course on how to be a reserve officer in the Army Medical Corps began. This presented a real hitch in my financial giddy-up.

Fortunately, I was offered a temporary position at a General Surgery clinic performing similar duties to those I performed when I worked earlier at the Baptist Hospital. But this time as a "doctor." Although it actually entailed the same physical activities, the "feel" was much different. I was not a medical school flunkie. It's amazing what a coat, tie, and your name preceded by the word "Doctor" does for your self-esteem. And, oh yes, with the title also came a little extra cash, which was desperately needed.

For George, having already served his time in the military, it was a completely different situation. He had arranged to stay on at John Gaston for an orthopedic residency. Molly had convinced him to postpone their wedding bells until summer, which she felt allowed her more time for appropriate "nesting."

Now, it was *adios*, and onward into the next phase. For me this occurred in early July when I reported to Fort Sam Houston, San Antonio, Texas. No parades, no bands, just "I'm here, here are my orders, where do I hang my hat?" A most undramatic beginning to the most dramatic change in my life.

A whole new world opened, one I never knew existed. My supposed two-year tour expanded by hook or crook to seven years. My "blend" I had been trying to find found me! While in the army I was offered an on-the-job short course in "everyday" Otolaryngology, that is, Ear, Nose and Throat, there being a shortage of such specialists in the medical services at the time. It fit like a glove, combining for me an ideal mixture of patient rapport and surgery. After I completed the four-month course, I applied and was accepted for a residency at a very esteemed army hospital. After leaving the army, I pursued an old passion, allergy, and later added otolaryngic allergy to my practice as a secondary specialty. It was primarily in this discipline I later became a researcher, teacher and author. In 1983 I was pleased to serve as the Prescient of the American Academy of Otolaryngic Allergy. Yes, as so often happens in life, my puzzle solved me instead of vice-versa. There is so much to say, so many tales to tell about those seven years in the service. I hope someday I have the opportunity.

In the meantime, back in Memphis the beat went on. Over the next twenty years or so, Memphis and John Gaston managed to co-exist without too many bumps in the road. By the late 1970s, however, as reported in the *Commercial Appeal,* January 13, 1980, Memphians' 1936 delight with their premier hospital had turned to dismay! After the usual cost debates, a new hospital was approved and a 1980s completion date announced.

The new hospital, the Regional Medical Center at Memphis, consists of a striking array of connecting pods, this time fronting on Jefferson instead of Madison Ave. The new University of Tennessee Health Science Center contributes a true complement to this new modern medical complex.

At least for hospitals, the "Sands of Time" seem to span a rather brief fifty years—everything, that is, but their memories. And, they're fading pretty fast!

BIOGRAPHY

William Payne King, M.D.

I was born on April 26, 1929 at Saint Joseph Hospital in Memphis, Tennessee. My father, William Sleigh King, was a podiatrist—foot doctor—in Memphis. Vintage-wise, he was more or less a Heinz '57 European-Caucasian product. While he had a nearby brother, his parents were separated, so he had no strong family ties. He was very active in national professional and local civic organizations, achieving high office in both.

Mother, Louisa Foppiano King, was sharply of Italian/English heritage. Unlike Father, her family ties were strong, especially to the paternal Italian half. While the Foppianos fit the mold of the typical large Italian family, the Paynes, from whom I got my middle name, were seldom in the picture. Because of physical problems she could have no more children, so all of her interests in life were directed to my father and me.

Though I was too young to realize it, those years after the 1929 Depression were pretty rough. We lived with my Foppiano grandparents the first few years of my life. My first recollections were of occurrences there. I recall at a very young age wearing a little sun suit and burning the bottoms of my feet on the hot summer concrete driveway. Also, when a little older, I recall playing under a large wooden round table on the screened-in back porch while my mother, sister and four brothers played pinochle over my head.

Before starting parochial grammar school, we moved into a small brick house a few blocks away. You know, one bathroom, a couple of bedrooms, and a front porch where we, like our neighbors, spent many of our summer evening hours visiting and cooling off. Of course, home air-conditioning was unheard of in those days, so when father installed a window fan we were, as said in the South, in tall cotton.

I distinctly remember our "icebox." Our icebox was a true "icebox." It required a block of ice, the latter being regularly delivered via tongs off an ice wagon that made daily rounds. We kids on hot days used to run behind the ice wagon to get ice slivers to suck on. What a treat!

Father drove the only car, a Dodge as I recall. I can still see mother walking a block down to the mom-and-pop grocery store on the corner in her rolled down hose and Father-insisted lace-up shoes. She would invariably return with two large brown paper sacks, one in each arm, both filled to the top with assorted groceries.

A couple of years before entering Christian Brothers High School, my father built a three-bedroom, one-bathroom house a few miles out on the then edge of town—the King family's abode until my father's death some twenty-six years later. Now, of course, the location is in the middle of "old town."

During my early grammar school days mother pushed her only child in the performing arts—singing and dancing. I can still remember the seemingly endless cutesy costumes and recital routines. In the last half of grammar school it was classical piano. All of which resulted in a now much-appreciated love of music and dancing.

With the advent of high school my love of sports took over. Though I participated in basketball and track, football was my thing. I physically developed early, so together with better-than-average lower body strength and coordination, probably a result of mother's dancing lessons, I was an all-Memphis tackle in junior high, and one of two three-year lettermen in high school. During this time I was also playing the piano in the dance band, singing in the glee club and double quartet, and generally having a ball. Grades came relatively easy, and the Memphis girls were truly belles. A broken collarbone mid-season in my senior year ended my pigskin career. In truth, while a pretty fair high school player, I had stopped growing and would have been fodder at the next level.

At that point, I wanted to stick my toe in new waters and seek college in some faraway strange land, like North Carolina—a practical compromise to some really foreign northern or eastern university. I was accepted at Duke University, to both my father's delight and financial chagrin.

I arrived at Duke on a very tight allowance, a former big frog in a small pond, now a small frog in a big pond. Not only was the atmosphere overwhelming, but also there was this unexpected cultural shock. While technically a Southern school, a large percent of the student body was from the northeastern part of the country. They spoke a different language! Where I came from their normal interpersonal conversations would have resulted in at least a fistfight. In retrospect, I'm sure I was an equally strange duck to them. But, alas, though it may require a slap in the face or two, we adapt.

I, naturally, chose pre-medicine for my major, and would have made Phi Beta Kappa had it not been for a couple of C's during my more unsettled freshman year. I joined a fraternity, Pi Kappa Alpha, and, along with other student activities, wrote music and lyrics for Hoof and Horn Club student musicals. In fact, in truth, my dream was to be another Richard Rogers. I and one of my fraternity brothers with whom I composed music were invited by another student musician to visit him in his home in

Scarsdale, New York. From there we pounded the pavement to New York music publishers for two weeks. Though fun was had by all, I returned to Duke convinced I had better stick with my chosen medical endeavors.

Other than being in the 1951 graduating class, two other monumental occurrences happened in my senior year. First, I pinned my future wife, who at the time was a fellow pre-medical student. My fraternity serenaded her outside her dormitory window with a sweetheart song my previously mentioned collaborator and I had earlier written. Second, I was accepted into medical school at the University of Tennessee in Memphis.

We were married on August 20, 1951 in my bride's, Ann's, hometown of Burlington, North Carolina. The ceremony was performed in a very small Catholic church. Catholics were sort of a rarity in that part of the country. Both families were in attendance.

After a short honeymoon at the Cloister Hotel in Sea Island, Georgia, I started medical school in September. My father added a small kitchen and sitting room to my old bedroom on the back of the family house. The resulting "apartmentium" served as our castle for the next five years.

My father had generously agreed to provide the same college allowance through medical school. Ann pitched in, utilizing her Bachelor of Science degree in Zoology to obtain a medical technologist position at a nearby hospital—during which she obtained a Medical Technology Certification while on the job.

During my senior year we had our first of four children, our only girl. A brief financial crisis resulted, but in those days doctors and hospitals were kind to starving medical students. I graduated a member of Alpha Omega Alpha, the medical school honor society, and stood first in my medical class quarter.

I then applied and was accepted for a one-year rotating internship at the University of Tennessee charity hospital, John Gaston, there in Memphis.

Having been deferred from the armed services while accomplishing my medical education, my next step after internship was into the U.S. Army Medical Corps at Fort Sam Houston, San Antonio, Texas, in July 1956. While there attending a six-week introductory session, a four-month course in everyday Otolaryngology was offered at Walter Reed Hospital in Washington D.C. The course was necessitated by an armed service shortage of Ear, Nose, and Throat specialists. I applied and was accepted. So, off we went.

I took it, I liked it, and, after appropriate consideration of all factors, I applied and was accepted for a residency in Otolaryngology there at Walter Reed. This required a return to Fort Sam Houston for a six-month Army Medical Service School course for regular army physicians. At the completion of the course I was awarded the Skinner medal for top grades.

Then it was back to Walter Reed for three more years of official residency training. As for payback, I had promised the army continued time in service year for year; that is three more years. The first two years I spent as Chief of the E.N.T. service at Fort Knox, Kentucky—chief of me until I finally got an assistant general duty medical officer the second year of payback time. The last year I spent back at Walter Reed as Chief of the Hearing and Speech Center.

While there I took and passed my specialty board examinations in Chicago, Illinois. At that time the Cuban missile crisis was in full swing. I recall the sermon there at mass on Sunday being about "when the missiles strike Chicago." When I got back to Washington I was informed that I had been assigned to a combat surgical unit on a small island off of Cuba, and was placed on twenty-four notice. I evacuated my family down to North Carolina, and waited. I never went.

By then the family had grown from three to five. With every change of duty station we had all moved—furniture, piano, etc. By the end of my seven-year career we had moved seven times. Our second child, the first boy, was born in San Antonio during the six-month course, and our second boy at Walter Reed during my last year of payback After all of this family shuffling, as much as I enjoyed my time in service, I decided to look elsewhere—at thirty-four with a still-growing family it was about time to stop starting over.

I, by then, had severed all the balls and chains connecting me with Memphis. I had enjoyed the freshness of environment and attitude in the southwest when we were in San Antonio. Another E.N.T. physician seeking an associate invited Ann and me to come to Corpus Christi, Texas, for a look. When you fly off in March out of ice and snow and land in warm sunshine on a bluebonnet-covered airfield, it's hard not to be impressed, especially if you are a Southern lad.

Corpus Christi was a beautiful little city of near 250,000 people, about the size of Memphis when I was growing up. I liked that. The climate was more to my taste, and it sat directly on a beautiful bay, with a real beach on the Gulf of Mexico only a few miles down the road on Padre Island. The hospitals were nice, and the professional atmosphere receptive. It was love at first sight.

I officially resigned my majoral commission and moved the family, I hoped for the last time, to Corpus Christi, arriving the first week of July 1963. Shortly after getting temporarily set up in a reasonable motel, stark realities hitherto unappreciated became woefully apparent. While the army provided housing, medical care, and a salary sufficient for the usual living expenses, with our family situation notable savings had been all but impossible. So, I arrived in Corpus Christi with a grand total of about $2,000 in the family treasury. I had been guaranteed a small monthly grocery/rent stipend until my earnings equaled that amount, which was anticipated to occur promptly. The only catch, much to my dismay, was that this city at that time had no suitable rental property. I couldn't believe it: no apartments, no acceptable houses for rent—and money was running out!

Fortunately, I was informed of a physician who wanted to move into a larger house and was anxious to quickly sell his present home. The home was a three-bedroom-two-bath modern house in a nice neighborhood. He understood my situation, personally lent me the money to cover the necessary down payment, and sold me the house. Though it was tight, we got the loan paid off promptly. This gentleman remained a close friend until his recent death.

The new professional association unfortunately didn't last—two well-meaning but strong-willed captains on a single ship. Literally on a shoestring I took over the practice of an older retiring E.N.T. physician. I started with two employees, a receptionist/secretary and a nurse—both of whom stayed with me through those toughest of times for several years. I still love and respect both of those dear ladies. But more about the office later.

In June of 1965 along came son #3. Quickly, the house became too small. Consideration was given to adding on, but that was felt ill advised because we would be over-building the neighborhood. We looked and found just what we needed, a house/hotel in a relatively new development—five bedrooms plus nursery, three and a half baths. After about four years in our beloved first house, we moved. Father passed away from a long-suffered cancer shortly before the move, and mother offered to contribute to the cost if there was a room for her—unnecessary but appreciated.

It was during the early years in this house that my thespian juices again began to flow. The Corpus Christi Little Theater was a couple of blocks away. I visited, expressed my interest, and wound up on the council and in a few shows. While musicals were my first love, I appeared in only one, my first show, *Pajama Game*, and then only in a small non-musical part. Sophisticated comedy seemed more my thing. I was in four more Little Theater productions, limiting myself to one a year. I did the doctor in *Generation*, Chuckles in *A Thousand Clowns*, father of the bride in *Plaza Suite* and the drunken husband in *California Suite*. I received for each a "Sammy," the local equivalent of an "Oscar." Probably my most enjoyable role was that of Oscar in a local dinner theater presentation of *The Odd Couple*. Do you detect a little Walter Matthau typecasting?

It was in August 1970 we experienced our first and, I hope, last direct hit by a severe hurricane, Celia. Not only was my mother living there, but also my wife's sister was visiting. It was upon us so quickly hardly anyone on our street evacuated. And good thing, because if we had not been there for constant maintenance, the house would have been inundated.

Water was pouring in between the roof shingles, through all our ceiling light fixtures, under the doors—it was a mess! I nailed our double front doors together with two-by-fours, the only way to keep them shut. As the winds shifted we were constantly opening and shutting different windows to equalize inside air pressure. If not properly attended, we could have experienced a similar fate as did my next-door neighbor. I was standing looking out my second-floor window when suddenly, to my horror, I saw their entire roof lift off their one-story house and land in the middle of the street! With all the pipes spewing water into the air, it looked like a decapitated chicken. I was greatly relieved to see my neighbors immediately run across the street apparently unharmed into another house. Without electricity we camped out on the back porch for the next seven days. All the fences were down, so the neighborhood got real friendly. We cooked over the gas fireplace, and listened to our battery-powered radio. I'll never take ice for granted again!

After a few years there mother moved back to Memphis to live with her sister Virginia, who was recently widowed and without children. In fact, the whole Foppiano clan was otherwise childless except for myself and two seldom-to-be-seen sons of one of the brothers. Mother and Virginia's situation in Memphis became impossible. I had to keep flying back there to take care of their health needs and other problems. Ann and I agreed it would be easier for all of us if we just moved them to an apartment nearby here in Corpus Christi, which we did.

We lived in that big house some twelve years, over which the kids grew and the practice flourished. As invariably happens, the kids started leaving the nest—college, marriage, jobs, etc. I decided if we were ever going to build our dream house, it was now or never. An architect friend designed a beautiful home overlooking Corpus Christi bay, which we built and occupied in 1980.

We were all devastated when Mother a few years later died from a sudden heart attack and stroke. Virginia managed by herself for a while, but her health deteriorated to the point she could no longer cope. We only had one child still living at home, our youngest, so we moved her into a spare bedroom. It was about that time our doctor started calling my wife "Saint Ann."

After a while unfortunately, Virginia's health reached the point of needing constant twenty-four-hour care—more then we could manage. We placed her in a nursing home near the office where I could visit her daily. Kidney disease finally took its toll.

Sports wise, early in Corpus Christi I played a little golf with my "rat pack" buddies—a name a number of us newly arrived physicians gave ourselves. But, soon time constraints made tennis a better option—besides, my "B" tennis was better than my "C" golf. After a blown-out knee, however, it was back to the golf course to stay. Once a mid-eighties shooter, better add ten strokes now.

We enjoyed our dream home for thirteen years. The older three married children provided us with six grandchildren, one girl and five boys. The remaining single son went off to college, and I experienced a detached retina. The latter caused some depth perception changes, significant enough for me to discontinue my surgical practice. Again, Ann and I found ourselves with too much house, and, now, too much expense.

Early in my practice I had added E.N.T. Allergy, a passion of mine since residency, and it, along with my regular E.N.T. practice, had flourished. I had long ago moved into new and larger quarters, complete with audiometric, eletronystagmagraphic and X-ray equipment, and an office laboratory. I had added a partner, and at one point we had three clerical employees, four E.N.T. nurses, four allergy nurses and a laboratory technologist. Now, the partner and the laboratory had gone. With the increased Health Maintenance Organization, et al, paper work, I still needed three clericals to supplement the rest of the staff, one full-time and one part-time E.N.T. nurse and three allergy nurses. With expenses ever rising, and insurance income persistently decreasing, the profit margin was steadfastly disappearing.

Bottom line, we sold our dream house and, in 1993, moved into a smaller town house, which we have thoroughly enjoyed. Because I loved my patients, staff, and practice, especially the allergy practice, I continued working at the office until early 2001 when a combination of financial realities and the failing health of both Ann and I forced the issue. I retired.

Here, I should thank God for allowing the two of us to do a good bit of traveling in our younger adult days when health was not a problem and the grandparents were available to keep the younger children. Thanks to pre-arranged, not too expensive, professional group tours, Ann and I saw a lot of this world fairly early in our lives. I learned a valuable lesson from my father, who was the more gregarious of my parents. Mother was a "blood is thicker than water," family-is-all person. It was Father who wanted to see and meet, and was going to do just that "one of these days." Those days never came. I listened and learned, and God provided the opportunities.

On one of these trips we had just arrived in Istanbul after three days in Romania, before we were to end our tour with three days in Dubrovnik. At three o'clock in the morning we received an emergency telephone call from my secretary telling me that Uncle Dee had suddenly died in his sleep! Uncle Dee, short for David, was the oldest of mother's four brothers. He had become ill in Chicago after his wife died. Since they had no children, the powers that be, whoever they were, deemed it appropriate to send him "home" to his family as soon as he could travel. This was when mother was living in Corpus

Christi, so guess who showed up at our airport commenting on the smooth "train" ride. He was obviously unable to care for himself and required constant observation, so we placed him in a nursing home—where he flirted with the ladies and seemed to thrive. Somehow, perhaps somewhat selfishly, I wasn't too inclined to rush home from Istanbul. My oldest son to the rescue! He accompanied mother with Dee's body back to Memphis for burial with the rest of the Foppiano family. Being the only available child in a large family can sometimes get a little burdensome.

Over my practicing years I was very involved in local and national professional activities. Not only was I a Fellow of the American Academy of Otolaryngology/Head and Neck Surgery, but also a Fellow of the American Academy of Otolaryngic Allergy, the American College of Allergy, and the College of Surgeons. After my required thesis was accepted, I also became a member of the prestigious Triological Society.

I contributed many articles and clinical research papers to peer-reviewed professional journals, as well as chapters in textbooks. I was elected President of the Pan American Allergy Society, 1978–1980. After serving on the council of the American Academy of Otolaryngic Allergy for many years, I became President of that organization in 1983. In 1995 I was awarded the President's Award by this Academy, and in 2001 a Lifetime Achievement award. In 1985 I was elected Chairman of the Board of Governors of the American Academy of Otolaryngology/Head and Neck Surgery.

Perhaps my greatest pleasure was derived from teaching. I gave countless lectures on Otolaryngic Allergy topics at basic and advanced E.N.T. Allergy courses across the country, as well as in Mexico and Australia. I served as Director of many of these courses. During these occasions I met a lot of brilliant and talented people, many becoming lifelong friends. If God sees fit, I hope to continue contributing from time to time.

Now that I am retired from my medical practice, I want to broaden my literary topics to anything and everything that strikes my fancy. My first book, *Follow the Green Line,* a tongue-in-cheek fiction-based-on-fact look at a medical internship at a large Southern charity hospital in the mid-1950s, was and is a lot of fun. The next, now in the research stage, is to be a semi-period novel about the lives of some unusually exciting people who actually lived and whom I personally knew. It's going to be a blast!